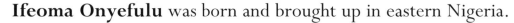

Ifeoma Onyefulu was born and brought up in eastern Nigeria.
After studying business management in London, she trained in photography
and then worked as a freelance press photographer. Her first book, *A is for Africa*,
was described by *Books for Keeps* as, 'like stepping from a darkened room straight
into noon sunshine,' and was chosen as one of Child Education's best information
books of 1993. Ifeoma has also written *One Big Family*, *Chidi Only Likes Blue*,
My *Grandfather is a Magician* and *Ebele's Favourite*, all for Frances Lincoln.
She lives in London with her husband and two sons.

EMEKA'S GIFT

An African Counting Story

IFEOMA ONYEFULU

FRANCES LINCOLN

To my parents Emmanuel and Emily, and to my son Emeka
for being a wonderful travelling companion.

Emeka's Gift copyright © Frances Lincoln Limited 1995
Text and illustrations copyright © Ifeoma Onyefulu 1995

First published in Great Britain in 1995 by
Frances Lincoln Limited, 4 Torriano Mews,
Torriano Avenue, London NW5 2RZ

First paperback edition 1998

British Library Cataloguing in Publication Data
available on request

ISBN 0-7112-0934-0 hardback
ISBN 0-7112-1255-4 paperback

Set in Perpetua

Printed in China

7 9 8 6

A Note from the Author

Emeka, the little boy in this book, lives in a village called Ibaji, in southern Nigeria, and comes from a tribe called Igala. The Igala people, who speak the Kwa language, are traders, farmers, fishermen and healers.

Most of the objects I have photographed are made by hand, with older family members passing on their skills to the younger ones. Some things are used every day: brooms to clear the compounds, hats for working out in the hot sun, pestles and mortars for pounding up food - a sound heard before mealtimes even in the cities. Other things are brought out on special occasions, like the musical *ishaka*, and the colourful necklaces women wear for important village events.

In many parts of Africa, grandmothers play a vital family role helping to bring up the children. When children visit their grandparents, they are often given a present, perhaps of homegrown fruit and vegetables - and sometimes the children give a present in return. As Emeka daydreams of all the things he could take his grandmother, he shows just how much he loves her.

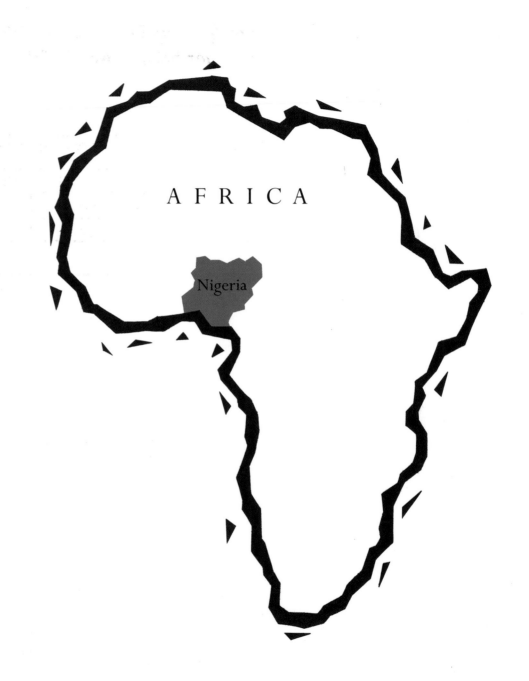

AFRICA

Nigeria

1

One boy who was not too small, but not too big either, set off to visit his grandmother in the next village. His name was Emeka.

Okoso

Children play this game with spinning tops, empty snail shells - or anything that spins. These girls are playing with a used pen top. The player whose okoso spins the longest is the winner.

2

Two of Emeka's friends, Bola and Ada, were kneeling on the path playing *okoso*, his favourite game.

Emeka smiled as he passed them, but he didn't stop because he was thinking, "What can I take Granny as a present?"

3

Three women on their way to market turned to say hello to Emeka. "There must be lots of things in the market that Granny would like," he thought, walking that way too.

Markets

Markets are important meeting-places for people from villages all around. The local chief is always there to act as chief official. As well as buying food, clothes and household things, you can get your hair plaited and your bicycle repaired at the local market.

4

Four new brooms were propped up against a wall.

"Wouldn't it be nice if Granny had one of those," said Emeka, "for sweeping away the leaves that fall down from the orange and mango trees."

5

Five children dressed up in big grown-up hats smiled and waved at Emeka.

"What lovely hats!" he said. "Granny might like one of those to keep out the sun when she goes to the farm or to market."

6

Six beautiful beaded necklaces were set out on display.

"My sister Oge wears beads like those," said Emeka. "Granny might say, 'Child, I am far too old for necklaces!' but I think she would look just as lovely as Oge."

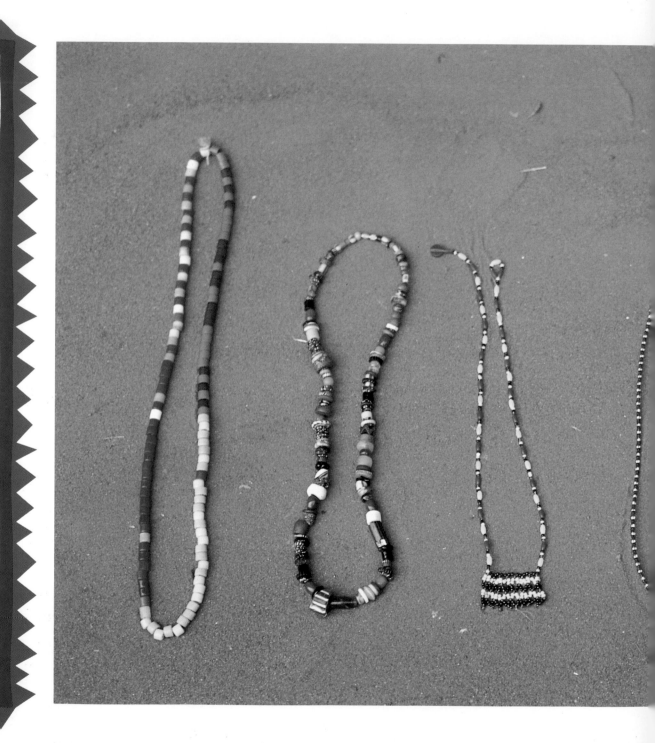

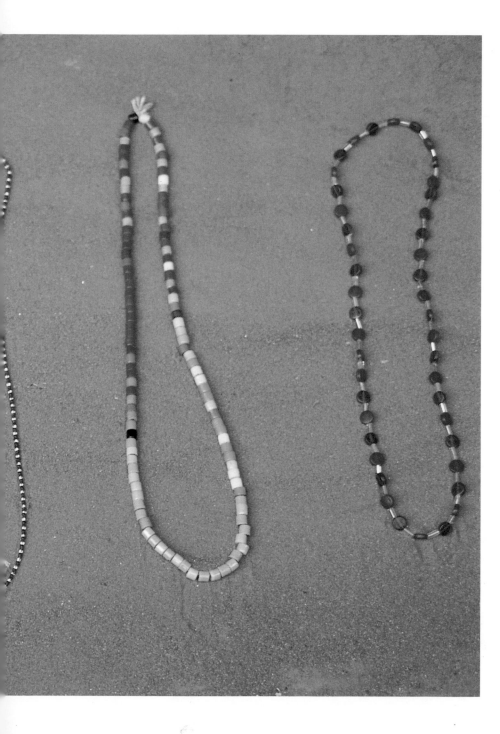

Necklaces

Young women and children wear them all the time, old women just for special occasions. Some necklaces are made from the dried seeds of the *akodegbe* plant, and some from glass or dyed rubber beads.

7

Seven musical instruments called *ishaka* caught Emeka's eye. Nearby, two girls were trying to play them like grown-up musicians.

Emeka laughed. "With those ishaka, Granny's dance group would be a big hit when they perform for the village."

Ishaka

These musical instruments are made from natural or red-dyed gourds hung with dried seeds from the akodegbe plant, or with pieces of cooked, dyed rubber taken from the rubber tree. Shaken from side to side, they make a distinctive soft, rattling sound.

8

Eight water-pots, some tall, some small, stood on sale by the roadside. Emeka looked them up and down.

"With pots like those, Granny could store water for days and days, and give the garden plenty to drink. Then her tomatoes would grow bigger than ever."

Water

In many African countries, the year is divided into rainy and dry seasons. People store water in earthenware pots, in plastic containers and in huge water tanks to use during the dry season, which lasts for several months.

9

Nine mortars and some pestles were lined up in rows at the end of the market.

"Some of those would be good for Granny's kitchen," thought Emeka. "Then, when I visit her with my cousins, we could help her to pound up yams for supper.

But with no money, I can't give her anything." He walked slowly up to his grandmother's house.

Pestles and mortars

Pestles and mortars are used for grinding up food. The wood-carver makes them from a tree trunk, hollowing out a piece very carefully to make the mortar. The pestle is shaped to make it easy to handle and to grind up different kinds of food.

10

Ten of Emeka's cousins were there, waiting to play with him. Emeka ran to tell his grandmother about all the things he wanted to bring her. But she just gave him a big hug, and said, "Child, you're the best present of all!"

Families

In many parts of Africa, a typical family household includes three generations, and the doors are always open to aunts, uncles and cousins - so there is someone to look after the children when the parents are out.

MORE PICTURE BOOKS IN PAPERBACK
FROM FRANCES LINCOLN

A IS FOR AFRICA
Ifeoma Onyefulu

From **Beads** to **Drums** to **Masquerades**, from **Grandmothe**r to **Yams**,
this photographic alphabet captures the rhythms of day-to-day village life in Africa.
Ifeoma Onyefulu's lens reveals not only traditional crafts and customs, but also the
African sense of occasion and fun, in images that will delight children the world over.

"An enchanting book with a positive and fresh perspective" *Junior Education*

Suitable for National Curriculum Geography, Key Stages 1 and 2; English – Reading, Key Stages 1 and 2
Scottish Guidelines Environmental Studies – Levels B and C; English Language Reading, Levels B and C
ISBN 0-7112-1029-2

ANANCY AND MR DRY-BONE
Fiona French

Penniless Anancy and rich Mr Dry-Bone both want to marry Miss Louise, but
she wants to marry the man who can make her laugh. An original story, based on
characters from traditional Caribbean and West African folk tales.

Shortlisted for the Kate Greenaway Medal 1992

Winner of the Sheffield Book Award 1992, Category 0-6 years

Selected for the National Curriculum English Key Stage 2 Reading List 1995 - 1997

Suitable for National Curriculum English - Reading, Key Stages 1 and 2
Scottish Guidelines English Language - Reading, Levels A and B
ISBN 0-7112-0787-9

Frances Lincoln titles are available from all good bookshops.